FREEDOM TO CHOOSE

E. L. Kidwell

KIDWELL
PUBLISHING

Table of Contents

Before the Beginning

In the beginning Elohim[1] created the heavens and earth.[2] But in the same week earth was created, Elohim—or simply God—also created many angelic beings that populated Heaven.[3] There were the cherubim, the personal guardians of God's Holy throne and worshiping onlookers of His glory, whose wings were so powerful that they sounded like the voice of the Almighty when He speaks.[4] There were the luminescent and majestic seraphim, the personal servants of Elohim, and constant singers of His goodness and holiness.[5] And there were many other creatures serving in the celestial kingdom, of such features that would make an adult shake with terror,

---

[1] Elohim is the plural form of Eloah, and is the Hebrew word used for God throughout the book of Genesis. Therefore, Elohim is used throughout this story as a form of address for the trinity as a whole.

[2] Genesis 1:1; Psalms 90:2; John 17:24.

[3] Ezekiel 28:15 describes Lucifer (and therefore all angels) as being created. John 1:2-3 describes all things made in the beginning by Christ.

[4] Ezekiel 10:5

[5] Isaiah 6:2-3

but of such gentle spirit that an innocent child would approach without fear.

In this realm of eternity, earth's Time was as strange a concept to the angels as Eternity is to mankind. There was no nighttime, for God's glory was a constant lamp to the Holy kingdom,[6] and therefore all "times" seemed like the day. Perhaps the only real aspect of time at work in eternity was the sequential occurrence of events. The angels viewed and understood events much like we understand the past, present, and future. In their minds, events had either already occurred, were currently occurring, or would eventually occur. But this time-like limitation was only upon the minds of the angels, and not the Maker Himself. Elohim was the most fantastic for His ability to comprehend all Eternity and Time as *the Present*—or simply *Now*. To the angels, they could see themselves as a single thread in the fabric of God's *current* design. But Elohim saw all the threads as they had been, were currently, and would eventually be— woven into His beautiful infinite tapestry. And

---

[6] Revelation 22:5

Elohim knew that as beautiful as this tapestry was in the realm before Time, it was still incomplete.

It seems contradictory to think of something that is perfect as being incomplete. After all, the very word *perfect* is a synonym of completeness by definition. But *perfect* and *incomplete* is how we must consider Heaven to have been. It was perfectly created, perfectly inhabited, perfectly governed, and perfectly maintained. And although the angels should have been grateful for the wonderful pleasures of having been created in a perfect environment, they had never known anything else. Could you fully appreciate a life without pain if you had never experienced pain? Would you be conscious of the perfect love of a perfect creator if you had never experienced the lack of love? How could the praises of your lips—the only gift able to be returned to a self-existent God—be expressed in gratitude for mercy received if you had never been in need of mercy? These were the threads that were missing: the voluntary love of creatures that had never experienced the glories of Heaven. The angels hadn't considered it, but in His all-foreseeing mind, Elohim was aware of this quality of embroidery that must bring the final adornment to His kingdom.

The Hosts of Heaven

Two of the archangelic chiefs were Gabriel and Michael. Gifted according to God's sovereign design, they excelled in their duties before God, and for His purposes. They were angels of action and assignment, the "minutemen" of Paradise. Theirs was the merit of usefulness and accomplishment of the will of God.

But no other angel compared in beauty or gifting to the highest ranking cherub in all of heaven, Lucifer. He was a creature perfect in beauty—his very name was derived from the word *praise*—and described him as a luminescent bearer-of-light. It was he who had the singular honor of covering the Lord Himself,[7] and leading Heaven's hosts into musical worship of their Master. As an ensemble of one, his music was glorious even by angelic standards. His distinction in Heaven was one of dearest love by his Lord and admiration by his peers. As of yet, this spirit was untainted by any evil, for no evil had ever existed.

---

[7] Ezekiel 28:12-15

He received true honor and respect by fulfilling his function of brining glory and praise to God.

There were many thousands of diverse angels occupying Heaven that demonstrated the different facets of God's creative ingenuity. One of the characteristics of God that is often overlooked is His perfect balance of sensibility with a sense of humor. This was evidenced by the great variety of the types and sizes of the angels the Lord had created. Some, like Lucifer, were intensely beautiful and clearly powerful. Others were more awesome for their hugeness, or more amiable for their happy faces with large smiles and tender eyes. Some seemed overly serious to those who seemed comical. Yet each angel was magnificent in beauty, and demonstrated the Lord's originality, art, and special touch of creative love; each was accepted as holy in the presence of the Lord, and possessed a heart-felt confidence that they were a vessel of the diverse splendor and honor of His creation.

Elohim had announced through the criers of Heaven that every angel must gather together for a service where He would be making an announcement of paramount importance. The meeting place was like a natural amphitheater, as if a gigantic bowl had been scooped out of Heaven's floor, or a mountain of space had grown upside down into an auditorium. The summoning of all angels to this most important meeting brought them together on the sloping terrain near the fringes, where crowding angels were conversing in small pockets typically consisting of those of equal or adjacent rank.

The angels' love for the Lord was unfathomable. And most felt their trust in His goodness invincible. But for the first time in their short existence they felt an uneasy sensation. There was a mystery about this meeting which suggested a parapet before their own consciousness and the knowledge of Elohim. It was as if the Lord knew something of such tremendous consequence that even these immortal beings needed divine protection and restrictions. They were aware that something new was underway, and the excitement of God moving in a way heretofore unknown pulsated in their celestial chests. The exhilaration of a fresh and unknown expression of the

Lord's power titillated the soul. The sheer thrill of divine innovation fused with the fear of change brought an energy into their beings as had never been known in eternity.

In one small group, Michael, Gabriel, and Lucifer were pondering these things in discourse. Michael, almost giddy with anticipation, exclaimed, "This is most exciting, is it not? Not once in all of eternity has Elohim called us together with such an air of expectancy! Lucifer, you're certainly the cherub closest to the Lord. Have you any knowledge of what cause the Lord might have to gather all the hosts of Heaven in such a manner?"

Lucifer had been staring aimlessly in what seemed to be deep thought about the same question. He gave a slight start, and answered with a smile, "Whatever it is, Michael, I'm sure it will reflect His deep and everlasting lovingkindness towards us, His angels. But, I admit that it is surprising that even I have not received any tidings of His Holy Secret."

Gabriel, also eager, replied, "It would appear that only the Father, the Son, and the Spirit themselves know for certain. But whatever Elohim is planning, I am beside myself with the expectation of good news!"

Nearby, four angels of lesser rank—we might think of them as *younger* angels—were also in conversation of these matters. (To call them *young* is not to say they lacked basic knowledge or ability, but that they had been created after many of the others. In eternity, all necessary abilities and knowledge are given to each angel at their creation according to God's sovereignty. There is not the progressive and infantile development which is evident in those constrained within time's dominion. At the point of their creation an angel is essentially mature, replete with knowledge, and completely capable of every good work.[8]) Two of these young angels, Aviel and Lain, had become instant friends, and had such close fellowship that many thought of them as if they had been created as celestial twins, kindred spirits and synergetic. They were the perfect picture of *philadelphia*[9]—or brotherly love—and blessed the heavens with their example of friendship.

---

[8] 1 Corinthians 13:12
[9] Hebrews 13:1

Also at hand was an affable angel named Kupal (though most called him Kupi for short). Kupi was most well known for his superlatively agreeable personality, and his oft animated interruptions. This gave him a special place in the hearts—and often in the ears—of the other heavenly inhabitants, and he was always lovingly tolerated if not enjoyed. You mustn't think Kupi to be willingly obnoxious. It was simply that his love for Elohim was so legitimate and sincere that he often forgot himself, thus leading to his outward absentmindedness. Truly, he even found a particular favor before the Lord, for his childlike faith and zeal were most pleasing to his loving Father of Heaven.

Another stander-by was the angel Adaiah. For all of the millions of angels in Heaven, many of them had not yet met, and this was in fact the first encounter Adaiah had with either Aviel or Lain. (But most agreed that it was unlikely to meet Aviel *without* meeting Lain, and vice versa.) Adaiah had already become well acquainted with and patiently patronized Kupi's company. They were considered to be friends, but of a different class than that of Aviel and Lain.

Adaiah and Kupi's relationship was one of *balance* as opposed to *enrichment*. Whereas Aviel and Lain fueled each other's mutual advantage, Adaiah and Kupi were like opposites that were necessary to prevent the other from self-destructing. Adaiah was calm, level-headed, and deliberate in his thoughts and speech. Kupi was excitable and exuberant. Adaiah was sensitive to the views and feelings of others. Kupi seemed carefree and careless. The two of them together were like a painting of Rembrandt, high in contrast and beautiful to behold.

As they were all in speculation of the Lord's upcoming declaration, Aviel enthusiastically said, "Perhaps He's going to create another Cherub or Seraph?"

Kupi interjected, "I agree."

Lain, more or less ignoring Kupi, replied, "There is such energy and excitement in Heaven, I can't help thinking that Elohim is going to reveal His purpose for bringing us forth. I feel like there's a purpose for my existence that I have not yet understood."

"I agree," said Kupi.

Adaiah said with a gleaming eye, "Maybe someone will receive a promotion!"

Kupi, holding up his index finger with a droll pedantic air, again popped in, "I agree."

Lain, possibly a little annoyed by his fledgling friend, looked at Kupi as to ask him to stop interrupting. But as was typical, Kupi's naivety considered Lain's expression to be an appreciative contemplation of his agreement, and was only the more encouraged. Aviel, acutely aware of the comedy before him, smiled and said, "Somehow I have some prescience that the ranks have already been assigned according to the qualities given us by Elohim."

"I agree!" declared Kupi.

At this point Kupi's zeal excited Lain, but not in the sense of a shared passion. It was more to the effect of a wound in Lain's sense of reason. Lain exclaimed, "Now hold on, Kupi! Adaiah thought that someone might be promoted, but Aviel believes that promotion is not possible. Then you agreed with both of them. How can you agree with both sides of a conversation?"

"Maybe I'm just agreeable," Kupi grinned.

Lain almost sounded impatient as he retorted, "Maybe you're just an…" Lain caught himself and smiled as he slowly said, "…angelic. But you always seem to agree with everything."

Kupi responded, "Not always." Then quickly realizing that he had actually disagreed with Lain, Kupi cried out with a sense of personal victory, "See!"

They all laughed as Aviel, Lain, and Adaiah said in unison, "Always."

Kupi smiled and said sheepishly, "I agree."

The Divine Declaration

As the appointed time for the meeting drew near, the heavenly hosts began to fill the holy hill. Some used their great wings to flutter and fly toward the front, and others filled the higher seats near the back. The rows were arranged by Heavenly rank, so that the highest officers were nearest the stage, with their direct subordinates immediately behind them, and so on. The arrangement was organized and orderly as is befitting for an assembly honoring God's Holiness. And Elohim's arrival would certainly cause this cloud of witnesses to fill the place with His praises.

One of the supernatural effects of Heaven is that neither sight nor sound are deteriorated by distance, but they are controlled by discretion. This is to say that far away sights and sounds are not experienced unless you give them your attention, and indeed they can be experienced if you focus upon them. Therefore, the angels toward the top of the auditorium were no less touched by the stage than those in the front row, although they had a less honorable situation.

Instinctively the angels took their places as they could feel the presence of the Lord was about to draw near. There was not an angel in Heaven that was not present, and there were none found tardy. Their profound love for their Master and solemn respect for His presence drew them like the welcomed love-call of a dove to its mate. The angels sat patiently, though they needn't wait for long, as they awaited the Lover of Soul's arrival.

In the very front was Lucifer, the Master of Ceremonies and leader of praise. Here functioning in his assigned position, the brilliance of his splendor was manifest in its proper caste. Never does a creature perform more excellent than when it ministers within its created purpose. And it was later to be that those who excelled within this confine were promoted to new offices with greater challenges and rewards. But is it not odd that those who believed themselves at the top of their grade were not always those promoted? In Heaven as on Earth, it seemed that the view of one's self was often less objective than that of the overseer.

But what of Lucifer? What advancement could he hope to receive? Even if he rose above all tendencies to mediocrity, even if he excelled to complete every mandate, even if he was *perfect* in his role, what promotion could be granted? As the Chief Cherub who covered God's throne, Lucifer was the highest official in all of Heaven—almost. As the leader of God's ministries, Lucifer was the director of everyone in Heaven—almost. His very rank was recognized by all to transcend all others—almost. Lucifer was first in command—almost. In fact, Lucifer was only *second* in command, *second* in rank, *second* in authority. In Heaven as on Earth, it seemed that those created to be *second* only doomed themselves by wishing to be *first*.

But Lucifer, yet maintaining some semblance of gratitude, did not dwell much on these thoughts. He was attentive to his duties, and faithful in his service for the time being.

Meanwhile, Elohim appeared near the stage, and the joyful movement of the community illustrated their adoration. As Elohim came on stage and took His place on the Holy Pedestal, Lucifer stood and called to the assembly, "All rise and praise the Lord, Elohim, the Father, Son, and Spirit, the Holy Trinity, the lover of all spirits, the creative and majestic God of Heaven!" The congregation was immediately on its feet, speaking in the tongues of angels[10] such a depth of praise and worship suitable for their hallowed maker. As a father receiving a gift from his beloved children, the Lord received their expressions of veneration with great joy; and looking upon the place with an omnipresent glance, each individual made personal contact with His eyes, and felt His love reciprocated. For an iota of time, Lucifer had taken his eyes from off the Lord, and observed the congregation. As a memory can be reviewed like a photograph, this image of adoring parishioners went through his mind. He stood on the stage near the Lord only slightly removed from the Pedestal. He imagined momentarily that Heaven's hosts were actually looking at him as they sung up their cries of

---

[10] 1 Corinthians 13:1

worship, and the new sensation pleased him. But these events occurred in such an infinitesimal instance that the ramifications of their presence were neglected. And though his eyes returned to the Lord, part of his heart did not.

Looking upon them compassionately, the Lord said, "Please be seated, and we shall begin." It should be observed that the Lord made no statement of gratitude, for to whom can the self-sufficient God of eternity rightly offer thanks? Is it not by Him that all things were made and do consist?[11] And if the Lord were to speak the words "thank you" to another being, it would be a contradiction to His own sufficiency. To any being subject to another, the necessity of gratitude is unambiguous. We are obliged for the subordinate services provided to accomplish our assignments, and we are empowered by authorities to undertake ventures beyond our capacity. We need each other, and therefore, gratitude is fitting if not requisite. No doubt it was obvious to the angels that God owed them no gratitude, for it

---

[11] Colossians 1:17

was they who were created by Him. He was the provider of every good thing, and for Him nothing could be granted that He could not supply for Himself. Nonetheless, the Lord demonstrated such abundant love for each of them that no question of His favor or goodness should have ever subsisted. Indeed, having beheld Him face-to-face, fellowshipped at His table, and listened to His voice, any question of His morality and justice should have been thrice removed. Perhaps the luciferous host of the event was simply becoming proud. He began to be like a sea creature that would not exhale. These creatures in the sea are able to glean breath from the surrounding waters, and this air within is compressed under the great barometric pressure it endures. Yet if the creature begins to ascend, even the smallest breath of air held as a bubble in the lungs will expand, increasing the creature's buoyancy, and accelerating its ascent. But if the beast is filled with the thrill of its promotion, and does not exhale the expanding air, that blesséd breath that elevates so quickly will eventually expand until it explodes the poor creature's lungs, and all will be lost. (It is clearly deadly for a sentient creature to allow its chest to become puffed up.) But if it contributes the breath back to the sea in a slow and constant exhale—enacting the steady and secure cycle of giving and receiving—all will be well. Though its climb is slower, it could never be surer. As for Lucifer, he held in the questions that began to bubble in the depths of his psyche, and the deadly effects of their forthcoming expansion would soon be inevitable.

The voice of Elohim was extraordinary, powerful, and like the sound of many waters.[12] Three distinct voices of different pitches came forth, but with the perfect timing of a single mind—a verbal orchestration of the most pleasant harmonies, a sound containing more grandeur and majesty than the sweetest songs of Lucifer. As all settled, the Lord began His declaration.

"I know that there is great anticipation and excitement in Heaven today, and so there should be. I have brought you here to impart my Holy Will. You are not merely my commanders and servants, but are

---

[12] Revelation 1:15

also my friends. Should I hide the thing that I do from you, my beloved spirits?

"We live in the spirit realm, in Eternity. Heretofore ours is the only realm of existence, and you are the only inhabitants of its goodness. It is my perfect will to create a new realm of existence which shall be called the physical realm."

If the significance of the underway speech had been any more momentous, to behold the expressions of joy and surprise upon the angelic mass would have been equally laughable. They were all visibly awestruck at the creativity of their King, and toward the back of the assembly was the vibrant Kupi smiling and quietly repeating to himself, "That's *perfect*! I agree! Amen! I agree!" The Lord continued His dissertation, and although He used words never before heard by the angels, the power of God gave them clairvoyant understanding as if the terms had been forever in their vocabulary.

"I will create a universe filled with galaxies, solar systems, stars and planets. Within the universe, I shall demonstrate my holiness by ordaining certain components of Creation as being holy. Each holy element will be for my purpose, my pleasure, or as my sovereignty desires. None may use it for other purposes than that which I have ordained, for it is set apart unto the Lord. Within the universe, one galaxy will be set apart, and within that galaxy, one solar system. That solar system will contain a planet that I will ordain as holy, which shall be known as Earth. Earth will sustain two basic forms of life called plant and animal. Of the plant life, one tree shall be set apart, which is The Tree of Knowledge of Good and Evil. Of the animal life, one species shall be set apart, which I shall call Man.

"Man shall be unique to all animal life, in that he will be created in our image to have authority over the Earth.[13] As ruler of the animal kingdom, I will give him an intelligent mind, a moral conscience, and most importantly an eternal soul."

The assembly was mesmerized by the news coming to their ears, and gave approbatory nods to one another, basking in the depth and greatness of the Lord's inspirations. The Lord, always the

---

[13] Genesis 1:27-28

gentleman, paused for the sake of His beloved friends and servants, and proceeded.

"I will personally have fellowship with Man, and he shall be able to love and worship me. I will to receive worship from a being that has never experienced the fullness of my glory through the senses of sight, sound, scent, taste, and touch. Therefore, another significant aspect of mankind will be that I shall give them a free will—they will possess the freedom to choose. In the day that they eat of the Tree of Knowledge, they shall surely die. Therefore, because of the great peril that mankind faces in their choices, and the faith that I will require of them, I have created you, My hosts, to minister to and to serve mankind throughout their life on Earth. You shall be their ministering spirits until they inherit their Salvation, and find their place as my children and joint heirs in Heaven."[14]

Michael and Gabriel immediately began to praise Elohim with superlatives that only heavenly immortals can invent, and the other angels followed.

---

[14] Hebrews 1:14

Then the Lord added, "He who is faithful in little, will also be faithful in much. Therefore, as men are brought from the physical into the spiritual realm, they shall be given great authority in my kingdom, and shall judge angels. And my love for mankind is so great that to touch them would be to touch the apple of my eye."[15]

Elohim having concluded, every spirit in creation seemed to be singing or praising the Lord wholeheartedly, except one. Lucifer, his visage slightly disfigured with confusion and jealousy, spoke up and asked with a subtle coyness, "But, Lord, why?"

At this, all of Heaven came quickly to silence, as this was a monumental event. Should the Creature question the Creator?[16] Though Lucifer began the tradition, mankind perfected it. And we did not heed the ancient lesson from Job, "Once I have spoken, but I will not answer."[17]

The simple question of "why" is like a palo verde

---

[15] Zechariah 2:8

[16] Job 40:2,8

[17] Job 40:5

tree, its existence sustained by deep roots fed by an unseen source. The secret fount of Lucifer's wavering heart was evidenced by this outwardly demure inquiry. No one in Heaven had ever before wondered about the Lord's motives. All He had ever done had been received in the simplicity and purity with which it had been given. But to those who are defiled and unbelieving nothing is pure; but even their mind and conscience are defiled.[18] Thus Heaven's Angel of Light began fading into darkness.

Elohim had not yet responded, and Lucifer presumptuously continuing with airs of modesty said, "Do not the praises of Heaven with my beautiful music more than glorify Your Highness?"

It is difficult, though not impossible, to hide our pride from one another beneath the surface of false humility. But what flaw can be hidden from an omniscient creator whose consciousness can penetrate not just the thoughts of a heart, but the intent behind the thoughts? The Lord was not deceived, nor could He ever be deceived. Yet, though

---

[18] Titus 1:15

His foreknowledge was perfect, He limited Himself to function within the linear limits of His Creation. He answered, "Heaven's praises are glorious, Lucifer. And nothing other than such thankful praise pleases my ears like your music. But My will shall be done."

The archangels begin to applaud, the others quickly joined in, and the reluctant Lucifer with conjoined applause and dissentious mind mingled with the rest. So it is with the most deadly deceptions of life.

Shouts of praise began to perfume the air.

"Praise the Lord!"

"Glory to the Lord!"

"Hallelujah! I agree!"

Elohim spoke, looking tenderly upon them and expressing His deep love for them all, and dismissed the assembly.

The Garden of Eden

It was a perfect day. Every day had been perfect, and it was likely taken for granted by the occupants of Eden that the days would always be perfect. A cleansing mist permeated the warm climate, and seemed refreshing to the young couple's exposed skin. Indeed they felt no shame, vulnerability, jealousy, or ambition in regards to one another. The harmony in their relationship was as sweet as Heaven's chorus. She was his perfect desire, and he was her unfailing security. For the first and last time in eternity, a man and a woman entirely and unreservedly loved, respected, trusted, and understood one other.

The man and his wife shared the common name of Adam,[19] and she felt no less for it. She was taken from the man, and loved him. And because she was a part of Adam nearest his heart, he indeed loved her

---

[19] Genesis 3:20. Eve did not receive a separate identity from Adam until after the fall.

like his own flesh.[20]

God had created within Adam a dissatisfaction with mere idle leisure, which is to say he had a very natural desire to occupy himself with work suitable to his frame. And so it was that the Lord's first gift unto the man was to give him a job even before He gave him a wife.[21]

The spirit of a person is seen in their work, or in their attitude towards work, and in all labor there is profit.[22] Consequently, for a man to refuse to work is to refuse the gift of dignity. All men desire dignity, which is correctly defined as having value or being worthy, and incorrectly defined as self-esteem. Many a lazy man will esteem himself highly, and blame his poor condition upon others. But his own estimation of his worth does not increase his value any more than fool's gold is worthy for its color. Dignity—or worthiness—comes to a man when he engages himself in the work for which he was created. This is why the Lord said to the man on the first day of his

---

[20] Genesis 2:23, Ephesians 5:28-29
[21] Genesis 2:15
[22] Proverbs 14:23

existence that he must tend the garden. In so doing, the Lord gave to the man the gift of legitimate and irrevocable dignity.

Every job has requirements and procedures, and one requirement the Lord had imposed was forbidding Adam from partaking of the fruit of the Tree of Knowledge of Good and Evil. For the Lord warned Adam that on the day that he ate of that fruit, "in dying you shall die."[23] It was not a warning of sudden or instant death. It was worse. Sin would cause death through *dying*, through suffering, through the gradual decay of aging and disease. The presumptions caused by misunderstanding this warning from God would soon be downfall of the young couple in Eden, and many others thereafter.[24] The warning was another gift from the Lord, given with mercy and love. In a word, it was the gift of a boundary. So long as Adam and his wife saw this boundary as a *blessing*, life was good. But Adam's self-will caused him difficulty,[25] and he tended to view this

---

[23] Genesis 2:16-17, original Hebrew is "*muwth muwth.*"

[24] Ecclesiastes 8:11

[25] James 1:14

boundary as a *restriction* instead of a *blessing*, as do most of his descendants. Although the blessing of boundaries should have been obvious to all succeeding generations, the youngest child to the oldest man still berates this virtuous gift of divine protection. Do not boundaries allow us to focus on that which we are able to accomplish, and neglect that which will fritter away our lives? If space contained air, would not man spend his wealth and energies to move there, and thus neglect his divine commission to tend the earth? If there were no rivers or oceans, would not men venture in conquest of lands near and far? If there was constant daylight, would not men seek to gain profit one score and four hours? Alas, the entire span of human history is the tragedy of men breaking the boundaries set by God, to the ruin of us all.

There were no natural predators in the world that were not subject to Adam. From the flea to the tyrannosaurus, or the mosquito to the pterodactyl, Adam was the master of them all, and to him they were as obedient and loyal as the best trained retriever. Indeed some of them even had voices, and were able to converse with mankind in a common language. This did not frighten or alarm Adam or his wife any more than you and I would be by a talking parrot.[26] Probably their tales of talking animals were commonplace for generations to follow, for even Balaam didn't start when conversing with the she-mule.[27] The young earth was as different from our older earth as the young child is different from the older man. It was pure, and therefore, it was lovely.

So it was that in six days time God not only created the universe with all its matter, but also male and female of every kind of creature. We must now consider how ludicrous it is to believe that asexual cells could evolve from electrically stimulated chemistry, and then that those same asexual cells could by chance develop into animals of different sexes. It is a magnificent religion—for it cannot be called proper science—that teaches that these gendered creatures not only magically developed—no one can prove just how—but they were able to find

---

[26] Genesis 3:1-2
[27] Numbers 22:29

food for themselves from the thousands of other gendered species that were also supposedly spontaneously generating around them. More incredible in that misguided faith is to believe that all of these couples evolved separately, and that all of these separate couples were able to find their proper mates! Of course, if the fantasy were to teach that a single pair developed first and all creatures followed from thence, that would be an even taller tale since they would both be feeding strictly upon plants, and none ever lost their mate. This would mean that the same bowl of shocked chowder would have had to produce two different cellular forms representing two different types of life: one with a cell wall and one without, and one that breathes oxygen and exhales CO_2 while the other breathes CO_2 and exhales oxygen. In all of my observed experiments, electricity not only damages or destroys life, and it has never *created* a heartbeat. Neither I nor anyone else has ever had a Petri dish of chemical stew give birth. Therefore, the theory of evolution is a religion of fantasy that has reversed the scientific method, and hindered human progress through its irrational faith in things it can never observe empirically. How ingeniously man strives to make himself more foolish.[28] So man has chosen to believe that he came from slime when indeed he came from dirt, and such groundless faith he requires of himself to avoid believing that he came from the ground.[29]

Back in Eden, every morning the Lord would meet and have fellowship with Adam,[30] as He still desires to meet with Adam's offspring every morning.[31] It was during each of these times of fellowship together that the Lord would reveal to them more of His own character and personality. The only way they could get to know and love Him better was if He would willingly speak words of revelation, and the only way He would speak to them was if they would have fellowship with Him. Although they were His own creation, He treated them with great respect and regarded them with dear friendship.

The Lord had said to Adam, "I have created you,

---

[28] Romans 1:22

[29] Genesis 2:17; 3:19

[30] Genesis 3:8: "In the cool of the day"; Mark 1:35

[31] Psalms 63:1

and I love you dearly. This garden that I have planted I give to you. Tend it and keep it.[32] Cause it to be fruitful. The woman I have given to you as a helper suitable for you.[33] Love her, cherish her, and protect her. Be fruitful together, and multiply. Fill the earth and subdue it. Have dominion over the fish of the sea, over the birds of the air, and over every living thing that moves on the earth. See, I have given you plants that bear fruits and seeds, and I have given you every green herb for food.[34] Of every tree of the garden you may freely eat, but of the Tree of Knowledge of Good and Evil you shall not eat, for in the day that you eat of it, in dying you will die."[35] Adam acquiesced with the reverence, love, and respect worthy his Creator, and it seemed that nothing would ever change.

---

[32] Genesis 2:8,15
[33] Genesis 2:18,22
[34] Genesis 1:28-29
[35] Genesis 2:16-17

Lucifer's Rant and Wicked Scheme

The certain path to losing sanity is to obsess over someone else's intentions, or to read into someone's actions a secret motive. Lucifer's speculation of Elohim's objectives (as if the Holy One could have any impurity in His reasoning), caused a subtle twisting to permeate his logic. He pondered secretly that God was a "hard man," that the Lord's intentions in creating angels was really just to enslave them! "How incredible," he thought, "that Elohim made the angels as mere servants, and His ultimate intention is for this filthy man-animal to be our master!" In his insanity, he began to believe that he had actually become enlightened to what he perceived to be the "cruelty" of God. "But this mustn't be known," he thought to himself. "Not yet." His timing would be crucial. "How ironic," Lucifer pondered, "that in the realm beyond *Time* that I should need *Time's* service?" But he used his magnificent beauty to hide his growing fury. Even in somber meditation, and no matter how wrinkled the brow, Lucifer shone with such a beautiful radiance that one could never wonder that he wasn't absolutely content.

The thing that caused such contrast between Lucifer's opinion of the Lord and those who were astonished at God's creativity was simply love. Those who trusted in the Lord's love also trusted in His goodness towards them, and felt no insecurity over the Lord's new mandate. They knew that their loving Father God could never be given to abuse, and no doubt of their own wellbeing entered their minds.

Lucifer, having felt slighted, was now isolating himself in Heaven.[36] He had long since justified his rebellion to himself, and was consumed by the frustration of his own inaction. His insanity did not consider the virtues of his wonderful home. Nor could he be satisfied any longer as the highest cherub over the Lord's throne. His existence in the most perfect environment was no defense against the deadly weapon of ingratitude.

---

[36] Proverbs 18:1

Perhaps the most incredible fact to be pondered was the Lord's scrupulous behavior as regards the gifts He had given. Lucifer was none diminished in skill or appearance, for the gifts and callings of God are without repentance.[37] Consequently, even Satan-in-the-making had not yet lost his glory. But it is a fatal error to believe that the Lord's goodness justifies our wickedness. Said differently, it is a faux pas to think that the fragrance of God's anointing upon a life is evidence of God's approval upon that life. On this slippery stone have many beings stumbled to their demise, of whom Lucifer was undoubtedly the first. So it was that the light that gave Lucifer his name was the only thing covering the darkness and shadows in his heart.

As Lucifer walked alone, privately nursing his hatred for mankind, a small group was nearby discussing the objects of his spite. He couldn't help overhear them, and slyly mingled into their midst. Among them were Aviel and his dear friend Lain. Kupi and Adaiah were also present, and listened on as

---

[37] Romans 11:29

Aviel had just begun to ask in an excited tone, "Have you seen them, yet?"

"Who?" replied Adaiah.

Lucifer strolled in with a sense of comedy to conceal his incense, and interrupted with a laugh, "Why, the monkeys, of course! Don't you just love the way they swing on vines, pick the insects from each other's hides, and throw…um…'stuff' at each other?" The angels laughed, protected by their own innocence. Aviel, still chuckling, answered, "I'm not speaking about the monkeys, I'm talking about mankind!" Under his breath, Lucifer said to himself, "So was I!"

Aviel continued, "They're magnificent!" Kupi, predictable to a fault began to interject, but Lain quickly put a finger in his face to shush him, and the angels all laughed again. Kupi said sheepishly, "Well, they are!"

Adaiah, still curious, said, "Of course, they must be! But, oh, how I can't wait to behold them myself!"

Mindful of the presence of an officer, Aviel asked, "Have you seen the new creation, Lucifer?"

"Oh, yes. Indeed I have," he coolly replied.

Seeking to continue discourse with such a prominent angel, Lain asked, "May you please expound upon what you have seen, Lucifer?"

Lucifer calmly responded, "Why certainly I may, and I'm so glad you asked." He began his rant in a quiet and superior tone, but progressing with a slow crescendo he began to betray the truth and falsehood within himself. He said,

"I've seen horses run on vacant plains,

Orcas swim in open sea,

Boars feed on sweet sugar cane,

Each of them wild, and all of them free.

The lion pride is calm and still,

The honey glistens in a hive of bees,

The black deep sea creature gets his will,

Each of them wild, and all of them free.

Wildfowl and owls take to open sky,

And insects nest within a tree,

Wolves howl in the moonlit night,

Each of them wild, and all of them free.

Elephants march through thick bamboo,

Rodents burrow in meadows green,

Sea gulls are soaring as they mew,

Each of them wild, and all of them free.

Gorillas play within their pod,

Sloths munch eucalyptus leaves,

But I think it rather odd,

Each of them wild, and all of them free?!?"

Lucifer was nearly shouting by the time he finished, and feeling the eyes of his beholders, he composed himself slightly, and mockingly added, "And I must say, I am impressed."

The angels had never experienced evil before, and were a bit dazed by this exhibit. But as is appropriate for subordinate officers, they would not touch the Lord's anointed,[38] and so they held their peace. Aviel decided to part saying, "That's intriguing. Well, Kupi and I have to report for duty. God be glorified!" Kupi, a bit confused himself found comfort in the parting salutation, and habitually began, "I ah...I mean...me too!" And they departed.

---

[38] 1 Samuel 24:6; 1 Samuel 26:11a

Lucifer now looked upon the visages of Lain and Adaiah with a certain hunger, the desire to dominate, the ambition of dictatorship. But no man or angel has ever been seduced by a harsh tongue and a severe look. Consequently, Lucifer's intellect and wisdom mastered his rage, and he attempted to deceive them with his caring words. "So what do *you* think?" he asked.

Adaiah, slightly junior to Lain, paused to allow his senior to reply, then answered, "I think it's exhilarating! God is moving, and humanity sounds magnificent!"

Lucifer rejoined, "Of course they are! And having been entrusted by 'The Big Man' with the freedom to choose, why, they're going to need *our* help in their weakness of faith...what do you think about that?"

Lain answered, "I supposed I haven't considered it much before now."

Lucifer asked, "And I suppose it's really not *that* important anyway. But, Lain, when you were created was anyone commanded to serve you?"

Lain replied, "Well, now that you mention it, I'm not sure. I suppose we were all expected to serve and help each other."

Frustrated though reserved, Lucifer questioned again, "But what if you didn't *want* to serve?"

Lain, now resenting the questioning underway retorted, "I was glad to serve my Maker, and any of His creation!"

At last, Lucifer found a weakness in Lain's argument and subtly combated, "Of course you were. Serving God is great. He is *perfect*, like His creation. And for that matter, I suppose serving *any* of His creation would be no different than serving Elohim Himself." Mocking and laughing as if at himself, Lucifer went on, "But that's a pretty thought! Imagine what it's actually going to be like serving mankind! Ha!" With a smooth transition between his schizophrenic personalities, Lucifer resumed the manner of the highest officer nearest to the Lord, and said as if he was revealing privileged information, "You know, since Elohim actually plans on making men rulers in Heaven someday, did you every realize that for all of eternity we're going to be serving…well…you know…an animal? I just hope they're house trained by then!" And Lucifer roared with laughter, but no one else did.

As with all gossip, these innocent hearers could not be unaffected. The spray of treason and lies had hit its mark, and Lain was visibly upset.

"That's preposterous!" barked Lain.

Adaiah, with a good-versus-evil struggle beating within his breast, was also shaken but too flustered and confused to speak.

Lucifer, ever the master of deceit, answered with devilish ridicule, "Well, as you said, 'Happy just to serve!' Of course, if *I* were on the throne, I'd never expect Heaven's holy hosts to stoop so low."

Adaiah, forfeiting his righteous efforts to overcome, exclaimed, "Maybe you *should* be on the throne!" And surprising enough, Lain did not refute his subordinate for this most offensive suggestion.

Lucifer, now completely in control of these unfortunates' destinies replied, "Now, now…let's slow down here. I don't want to make any waves…*yet*. But perhaps we can talk later, amongst *friends*?" The intonations of his last word suggested that this could possibly have been the first invention of redefinition, for he seemed to mean *enemies*.

Lain being twice emboldened exclaimed, "Yes, I think we should!" And they made their fiendish plans.

As Lain and Adaiah departed to spread the lewd rumors they had received, Lucifer discoursed with himself.

"Now the seed is planted in Heaven. I must turn my attention to Earth. The very freedom that God has given man, I shall use to his undoing. God loves man. I hate man! I will turn the very creatures the Father loves against Him! Ha ha! The animals on Earth will turn *from* Him, the angels in Heaven will turn *on* Him, and I—yes I!—will have the throne!"

The Fall of Man

As Heaven's chief musician fell into dissonance, he disdained the harmonious trio of Heaven, and the counterpoint duet of earth. Having no power over the triune Elohim, he focused his attention on Eden's pair, and was intent on reducing their harmony with God and each other to a staccato tritone. He had no intent of joining in their orchestra, but rather of usurping its conductor, and thereby replacing the joyous scores of love, provision, and confidence with his own compositions of hatred, want, and insecurity. The metaphor is complete, and its success can be seen within a stone's throw of your own abode, if not within its very walls.

Adam was lying on the thick green grass in repose, for the garden seemed calm, and he felt absolutely secure in that delightful place. The grass was tall with broad blades the size of small feathers, and was not so stiff as to be abrasive. It was such a bed for Adam as you and I might compare to a pillow top mattress and down pillows. He was relaxed and leisurely passing the time, and had apparently neglected that solemn command of the Lord to *subdue*.

Why would the Lord order Adam to bring a perfectly created world under subjection? If it was created perfect, wouldn't all creatures be set in their proper caste? Most human minds consciously think of perfection as the absence of flaws, which is but one of the true definitions. But in God's creation, beings are perfectly created yet also possess free will. Therefore, it is possible for a perfect creature to destroy its own perfection *with* its free will. This means that things are not necessarily governed by one single truth, but by an array of truths that can function independently, harmoniously, or synergistically. For example, a carpenter might create a two-legged chair which would obviously be an imperfect creation since it lacks the balance necessary to make it useful. Any dunderhead that dared used it would probably end up resembling a rum-struck sailor in a tempest, and once he regained his bearings he might shower his drunken blessings upon the senseless woodworker. But if that carpenter were to create a four-legged chair, *that* would be a perfect, balanced, and functional creation, possibly even able to uphold our teetering friend or a teetotaler alike. How then if the carpenter possessed the power to give his perfect chair a sentient free will, and of its own will—however misguided—the chair damaged two of its own legs? It is no longer perfect, however perfect it was created. The carpenter is not to blame since the chair of its own free will has destroyed its own perfection. So it is with mankind: perfectly created, and willfully imperfect. Then, how much worse is it when man curses his Creator for his own self-inflicted imperfections? Or when God is blamed for the vices and crimes of fallen men? Is the Creator to blame for the choices of his free creatures? Is it not the summit of hypocrisy for us to use our free will to condemn the Creator that gave us our free will? Would we, too, make God seem evil in order to make ourselves seem good?[39] The answer, of course, is yes. We all do.

---

[39] Job 40:8

Adam had tended the garden, and having completed a portion of the work assigned, he reposed himself leaving the rest undone. So unsubdued, the garden blew to and fro in comfortable breezes. As Adam lay in the grass he glanced towards his wife, and noticed what you and I would probably have called a snake-like dinosaur, or perhaps a dragon. It was serpentine in figure, and yet walked about on legs—like the dragons in ancient China and Korea as depicted in their art. The Serpent glanced at Adam, and made a subtle bow of the head as any subject might make to his king whether he was truly subjected to the king or not. Something in Adam half-suspected the beast of offering the obeisance as a mocking jest more than in sincere respect. But Adam was too comfortable to move, so he lay back and closed his eyes, but kept his ear upon the Serpent's voice as it continued to pass, speaking to the wife.

"Good afternoon, my Dear Queen!"

Adam's wife looked up with an innocent smile, "Hello, Serpent! What have you been doing today?"

"Well, I've just been strolling through the center of the garden."

"The *center*!" she exclaimed. "You mean near the *forbidden tree*?!?"

"Of course!" said the devilish beast. "I didn't *eat* it, though I must confess I thought the fruit looked especially delicious."

The woman's eyes grew wide, and she could hardly help admiring the brute for his boldness, though she shuttered at the thought of the tree.

"*We're* not allowed to get near that tree. Elohim said so."

Adam's ears continued to listen, and yet he continued to be unmoved, and failed to protect his wife from this fiendish interrogation.

Pleased by this rapid progress, the Serpent asked the Question that he knew would confuse this poor spotless mind, "Has Elohim indeed said that you shall *not* eat of every tree of the garden?" Simply negating Elohim's statement with the world "not" would have certainly caused suspicion even in a mind as virtuous as Adam's wife. But to negate Elohim's statement within the Question was as cunning and diabolical a trick as the world had never experienced up to that point.

What power is there in the question mark? What power is there in the question mark! The straight and narrow exclamation point offers unobscured boundaries of right and wrong! But what power of evil takes hold when the straight and narrow is made crooked? What wickedness in men causes us to ponder the moral questions that have been obvious to so many generations before us? A question! A question that required no response! A question that did *not* have to be pondered! A question that did *not* have to be solved! A question of obvious moral solution that was pondered instead of pummeled! It was such moral questioning that led men from God. It was such moral questioning that severed marriage. It was such moral questioning that murdered civility. It was such moral questioning that exalted the creature above the Creator.

The Serpent's question caused the woman's mind to slightly reel with confusion—a phenomenon that in-and-of-itself was troubling to her—and her untrained innocence suffered to ignore the seeming trifle. But if the woman's psyche had ever been blemished with sin, she would have recognized the stain in another. Although her intellect was keen and brilliant, her discernment of this wicked spirit was blind, and as the woman who rode the tiger,[40] she continued oblivious to her own danger. "We may eat of the fruit of the trees of the garden," she said, "but of the fruit of the tree that is in the middle of the garden Elohim has said, 'You shall not eat it, nor even touch it,[41] or else you will die!'"

An evil spirit cannot be reasoned away with the intellect any more than a storm cloud can be moved by a hand fan. Thus it was that this devil-inspired Serpent was fortified by the woman's reason, and darted his fiery lie into the very heart of the woman's soul. With a comforting laugh he said, "You will *not* surely die! For God knows that in the day you eat of it your eyes will be opened, and you will be like God, knowing good and evil."

---

[40] An anonymous limerick reads:
There was a young lady from Niger
Who smiled as she rode on a tiger.
They returned from the ride
With the lady inside,
And a smile on the face of the tiger.

[41] Eve incorrectly quoted God, possibly because this is what she had learned from Adam.

The woman had never before felt this emotion that was now swelling within her, and the thoughts that accompanied it were anything but rational. She was now beginning to question her own knowledge, to judge her own worth, and to ponder the Serpent's lie. This new emotion was one of the most detrimental to the human race, and what we today call insecurity. If Adam would have subdued the Serpent in the garden, he may have understood how to subdue the monstrous sentiment growing within his wife's heart. But in willfully ignorant bliss he stayed reposed in his own selfish comforts. Without confidence in herself, her husband, or her God, the woman walked with the Serpent towards the center of the garden, and began to stare at the fruit that for so long had been forbidden, and yet now seemed so inviting. She continued to ponder the Question and the Lie. The Question: *What* did God say? The Lie: *I* can be like God. Question. *What?* Lie. *I. What?* *I.* Question. Lie. *I...I!* With these thoughts reverberating in her mind like the crash of broken glass, she continued to examine the forbidden tree and its fruit. The longer she stared the more she began to think it not so deadly after all. She began to hunger for it. She began to be attracted to its beauty. She began to desire its wisdom.[42] She reached out to touch it, and involuntarily jerked her hand back at first contact. She thought, "I *touched* it, and I didn't die! Didn't Elohim say that if we *touched* it we would surely die? And I touched it!" In reality Elohim had never said any such thing, and so—as is always the case—an error in her knowledge of God fueled the error in her actions. Now twice emboldened she reached out again, grabbed hold of one of the luscious fruits, but only held it in her hand without picking it from the tree. The branch resisted her grasp on the forbidden fruit, and in one last act of mercy tugged against her efforts at sin as her own conscience was tugging at her heartstrings. But she began to feel a sense of bravery at these shameful actions, and with a quick jerk she pulled it down and stood there with it in her hand. She lifted it to her lips and breathed in the sweet aroma. She felt it was too late to turn back now, and she hastily bit into the fruit

---

[42] 1 John 2:16

to prevent herself any repentance. She savored its juices with every awakened sense, and happily swallowed sin and death into the depths of her being. She turned toward the serpent and commented, "You're right! It *is* delicious!" But the serpent was gone. Where had he gone? When did he leave? Why? Questions. All that remained of their discourse was questions.

Now alone with her thoughts she began to feel a new instinct at work. For the first time in her life she felt afraid. She never took time to consider this new emotion of fear, but only reacted to it. She looked at the bite mark she had made in the forbidden fruit, paused, and ran to her husband. She awoke him from his lazy stupor, and recounted the success of her adventure with the forbidden fruit. She showed the unfinished fruit as evidence of her story. She had never had to *prove* anything before—everything spoken had simply been *understood* to be *true*. But with sin came suspicion, and she felt obliged to justify her tale. It was now, at this very moment, that the greatest tragedy of all time took place. Instead of saving his wife from sin, the first man surrendered to it. She had been deceived, but he knowingly received the forbidden fruit and ate.[43] Perhaps he thought he could be her salvation. Perhaps he just wanted it. Whatever his reasons or excuses, the only fact that mattered now was that the first Adam sinned.

There was no immediate physical change that could be perceived, but if they could have seen the spiritual realm about them they would have trembled in their own failure. Though naked in the body, in the spiritual realm they had appeared fashioned as a glorious King and Queen of the Earth. Now they stood with arms outstretched in the shape of a cross, a prophecy of death from sin. They were clothed from shoulder to the ground in the most beautifully rich and whitest of robes, adorned with golden crowns, and embellished with precious jewels.[44] The hideous spirit of Sin approached, and in the glorious presence of these Majesties, Sin appeared the more vile and appalling. It savagely ripped their crowns from off their heads, and at its touch the crowns

---

[43] 1 Timothy 2:14
[44] Isaiah 61:10

melted into powder even as an old dry orange is dissolved by mold. Sin stripped them of their robes with a violent tear, and their robes burned into a pungent black smoke which fell upon their spirits as an unwashable stain. Sin clawed and wounded these poor souls, and as the essence of their spiritual life began to bleed out of them physical death was now imminent.

The couple had been *physically* naked without shame, and had not realized this was because they were wearing *spiritual* garments. Their confidence, their peace, and all of their joy had been the result of the unseen covering of their souls. With that covering removed, they desperately sought a substitute to hide the disgrace they each felt in the presence of one another. The best they could do was to sew fig leaves together,[45] and it was clearly not enough.

Mankind was lost. The Earth was lost.[46] And yet God still came to have His daily fellowship with Adam. The Lord's voice could be heard calling throughout the garden, "Adam, where are you?"

---

[45] Genesis 3:7
[46] Romans 8:22

Never before had the omnipotent voice of Elohim asked a question, for the omniscient mind of Elohim possessed all answers. He knew *where* they hid, and He knew *why* they hid, but in His perfect love He sought for willing repentance, and not righteous judgment.[47] The man and woman would not quickly come out from their hiding place for the great shame that accompanied their sin. They slowly came forth clothed in their self-made coverings, and Adam confessed his fear and nakedness. The Lord questioned him about the tree. So many new feelings pounded in his heart he could hardly control them, then impulsively he exclaimed, "It was the *woman* that *You* gave me! She gave it to me, and I ate!" Sin had reduced this man—a man who had once been responsible and decisive enough to name all the animals in one day—to such contemptible depths of cowardice as to throw the damsel into the train to save his own wretched skin. And the man felt the embarrassment caused by his own diminution. Never before had his eyes drooped, nor his head hung, nor

[47] Hosea 6:6

his face frowned; but now all dignity was gone. The woman also confessed, "The Serpent deceived me, and I ate!"

To the Serpent the Lord would ask no questions, for no confession of the serpent would be offered any forgiveness. The spirit of the serpent was eternal in nature,[48] and therefore faith was impossible. And since God cannot be pleased or appeased without faith,[49] God cast His eternal judgment upon the wicked fiend.

The couple's knowledge and understanding had been limited to the realm of Time; and despite their intimate relationship with the Lord, they still required faith to trust Him. Therefore, Elohim had ordained that He would pardon the sins of men through a sacrifice of blood, and so he slew a lamb and made for them coverings of skin.[50] So although their bodies would still die, God redeemed their souls from death. Lucifer's plan to keep mankind from Heaven had failed, and his rage could no longer be contained.

---

[48] Revelation 20:2
[49] Hebrews 11:6
[50] Genesis 3:21

And There Was
War in Heaven

Heaven had been created and governed by Elohim as the perfect dwelling place of all eternal spirits, including the souls of mankind. But even as joy cannot be taken from a perfect heart,[51] it cannot be received by an imperfect one. So despite Heaven's perfections, the proud heart of Lucifer would not be satisfied. Greatness is always held in contempt by the proud, so the greatest symbol of the greatest greatness was hated with the greatest contempt by him with the greatest pride.

In the throne room Elohim sat upon that sacred seat so coveted by Lucifer. The deception of man was no secret, and the true servants of God were subdued to think that the objects of the Lord's deepest affections should so wrongly abuse His mercies by so quickly disregarding His commands.

Aviel and Kupi sensed the coming danger, and

---

[51] John 16:22

yet, felt at peace in the Lord's presence. Aviel was patient yet alert, ready to jump at the first command of the Lord. Kupi's personality now revealed a deep courage that had never been seen when it was not needed. There was still an echo of the youthful exuberance and amiability, but more prominently visible was a confident bravery that would make the mightiest of men shudder to face. Like the mother bear that is good natured until her young are threatened, the happenings of Heaven had now revealed in Kupi a terrific warrior of God.

As the Father spoke, all others fell silent.

"As it is written, Lucifer has betrayed us, and Man has fallen. I would not have one soul to perish, but that all would come to repentance.[52] But without the shedding of blood there is no remission for sin."[53]

In their perfect fellowship and unity, the Son answers the will of the Father, "Yes, Father. I will go. I will give my blood that man may be saved."[54]

Then spoke the Holy Spirit, "Yes, Son. I will

---

[52] 2 Peter 3:9
[53] Leviticus 17:11; Hebrews 9:22
[54] John 10:17-18a

touch the conscience of man, and draw on them to repent."[55]

The Father replied, "Yes, Spirit. I will send my Son into the world, not to condemn the world, but that the world through Him might be saved. He who believes in Him is not condemned. But he who does not believe is condemned already, because he has not believed in the name of the only begotten Son of God.[56] In the fullness of time all shall be done.[57] But behold! Lucifer's rebellion is not yet complete."

Then with a thunderous shout, Elohim cried out, "Lucifer! Come here now!"

Before this point, few in Heaven had witnessed the awesome power of the Word of the Lord. Lucifer entered the throne room as though struggling with some unseen force, and all realized it was the power of God's Word that had removed Lucifer's freedom. They knew that Elohim had spoken the worlds into existence,[58] but now understood that every good

---

[55] Romans 9:1; Hebrews 9:8-9
[56] John 3:17-18
[57] Galatians 4:4-5
[58] Genesis 1:3, 6-7, 9

aspect of their existence had been gifted to them by their Creator, and therefore, He had the right and responsibility to take it back at His pleasure. Those possessing this revelation would later become known as the Wise, both those among the angels and those among men.

Lucifer had not been fulfilling his duty of covering God's throne, thus Gabriel and Michael rendered service nearest to the Lord. They stood at the base of the throne with their flaming swords in their hands.[59] Indeed, all of the angels in the throne room had drawn their swords in response to their sergeants.

Lucifer's hatred seethed from his person like the infection of a boil. Gabriel and Michael, rushing at either side of Lucifer, grabbed his arms as if to restrain him. He growled in proud anger to be seemingly withheld by those previously his subordinates, yet was momentarily distracted, frustrated, and confused by his loss of free will. Elohim stripped him of the once-glorious name of

---

[59] Genesis 3:24; Numbers 22:23a

Lucifer, and at the same moment ordered this fallen being to give an account:

"What have you done, Satan?!?"[60]

Satan was now temporarily released by God from the power restraining him so that he might freely confess. He roared like a lion,[61] and threw Gabriel and Michael to the ground with each arm.

"I owe You no answer!" he screamed. "The question is what have *You* done?!? *You* have doomed Heaven to be corrupted by those mangy mutts of Earth! *You* have reduced the glory of angels to the dust! *You* have deceived us by pretending that You are Love! If You are Love, then I hereby am Hate! If You are Good, then I am Evil! If You are Ally then I am Enemy! The name *Satan* is the last thing I will ever accept from You before You are destroyed! And coming from You, I hold the name *Adversary* as dear as the greatest compliment ever given!" Then calling to all the hosts of Heaven, Satan cried out, "All who are with me, attack!!!"

---

[60] *Satan* is a Hebrew word, and literally means *adversary* or *enemy*.
[61] 1 Peter 5:8

And there was war in Heaven.[62]

Flaming swords began to fly. The friends of God were surprised to see so many of the other angels joining Satan in his ludicrous revolution.

Among the ranks of hell, there fought Lain. His occasional impatience had become the root of his fall, and so it seemed fated that he should cross swords with Aviel, the picture of patience among God's faithful spirits. Aviel, torn between the love of his bosom friend and the lover of souls, fought within himself even as he battled for Heaven's sake. Between the two, Aviel was by far the superior warrior, able to choose his blows with precision while Lain would use all his energies by attacking pell-mell. As Aviel would strike Lain, and Lain would pause to recover, Aviel would plead with him, "Lain, we were brothers! We had sweet fellowship together! The closeness of our friendship was a rarity even among the angelic!" Lain would recover himself and charge, screaming his chant like a lunatic, "I know no love! To live is hate! I know no friends! I will not wait!" And as they fell to it

---

[62] Revelation 12:7

again, Satan felt a perverse sense of triumph to have sown discord among once united brethren.[63]

Adaiah had also joined with the rebels, and the subtle pride that had once intrigued him with promotion had now demoted him to a demon of hell. How fitting that he should be battling with Kupi, perhaps the most humble of the angels. Because Adaiah was so sensitive to insults against himself, he thought that he would find the same weakness in Kupi. He used his belittling words as a sword,[64] and said, "Kupi, you are the most pathetic of spirits, and a perfect example of Elohim's imperfection!" But Kupi retorted, "When I am weak, in Him I am strong!"[65] which struck Adaiah to the liver. Adaiah counterattacked, "None of the spirits like you, and even those of Heaven merely tolerate you for fear of judgment!" But Kupi's faith in God's goodness made him victorious in his assault as he replied, "I would rather be a doorkeeper in the house of my God than

---

[63] Proverbs 6:14, 19
[64] Psalms 64:2-3
[65] Hebrews 11:34

dwell in the tents of wickedness!"[66] And his grace and skill in battle eventually pinned Adaiah between the wall and the sword, for pride will always be overcome by humility in the end.

Throughout Heaven there fought the spirits of all sin, and their godly counterparts. Jealousy fought against Trust. Shame combated Forgiveness. Lust battled with Love. Stubbornness brawled with Obedience. Some of the sinful spirits were so foolish they even attacked one another on occasion. Arrogance smote at Ignorance, and Drunkenness struck Materialism once or twice although they were trying to fight together. The demons could neither restrain nor bring order to the chaos loosed by their own rebellion.

Satan brandished two swords, one in each hand, and was battling against both Gabriel and Michael. Being created to cover God's throne did not come without its perks. Satan was a master swordsman, and was rapidly alternating his attacks and parries—even simultaneously—against his two opponents. But as

---

[66] Psalms 84:10

Gabriel and Michael fought side by side, they were able to hold the devil at bay, and to inhibit his progress.

Satan was attempting to work towards his prime objective, the throne, where he insanely thought he could face Elohim in combat.

Elohim sat at such peace on the throne that one might think He wasn't aware that His kingdom was engulfed in a war. But that was far from the truth. In reality, the God who gives peace *is* Peace. So no form of unrest could cause Him any anxiety, even if hell itself were at war on His doorstep—and it was.

Injuries were inflicted on both sides, but none so terrible as upon Heaven itself. The once peaceful air now rang with the clashing of swords, the courageous battle cries of the Lord's loyal army, and the bestial growls of the fallen. Life and love seemed under threat. Paradise seemed lost. And the Lord seemed to be letting it.

As the angels toiled in their warfare, some wondered how long this battle would continue, and if the Lord was ever going to intervene. Suddenly, from the throne came a voice of thunder.

"Enough! Enemies of Heaven be still!"

The battle instantly stopped on all fronts, and Satan and his demons stood consciously frozen by the almighty power of God's speech. Then, for the first time in eternity the angels began to understand that Heaven is only reserved for those of resolution—men and spirits alike—and not the demonically double-minded.[67]

God spoke again, "He who works deceit shall not dwell within my house, and he who tells lies shall not continue in my presence."[68]

The angelic spirits had never before seen the wrath of God fall upon anyone or anything. But there was no mistaking the deep anger and displeasure in His voice now.

"Satan! You and your demons are hereby banished from Heaven, and cast down to Earth like lightning!"[69]

God again demanded an account from Satan, but this time God's power seemed to force Satan to

---

[67] Isaiah 50:7
[68] Psalms 101:7
[69] Luke 10:18

respond to His interrogation. As the Lord questioned him, Satan's free will was temporarily lost, and his inner being had to shout out the evil words previously kept within.[70] Thus proceeded God's prosecution and Satan's confession:

"For you have said in your heart…"

"I will ascend into Heaven!"

"And you have said in your heart…"

"I will exalt my throne above the stars of God!"

"And you have said in your heart…"

"I will ascend above the heights of the clouds!"

"And you have said in your heart…"

"I will be like the Most High!"

The evidence presented, Elohim proceeded to cast His righteous sentence, "Yet you shall be brought down to Sheol, to the lowest depths of the pit! Those who see you will gaze at you, and consider you saying, 'Is this the man who made the earth tremble, who shook kingdoms, who made the world as a wilderness and destroyed its cities, who did not open the house

---

[70] Luke 6:45

of his prisoners?""[71]

Now a frightening change came over Satan and his followers. Their white robes transformed into filthy rags, and their once-beautiful countenances became odious.

As the Lord raised His arm to finalize His judgment as with a gavel, Satan realized his utter defeat. Satan felt a sudden terror gripping him as he understood his imminent sentence was about to take place. But in the madness of his pride, Satan defiantly shouted out, "I will have my revenge!" The Lord's arm fell rapidly, and in a flash His sentence was executed. Heaven was instantly cleansed and purified.

Elohim spoke, "Now is the time when true believers will worship me in spirit and in truth."[72]

In a loud voice someone proclaimed, "Now salvation, and strength, and the kingdom of our God, and the power of His Christ have come, for the accuser of our brethren, who accused them before our God day and night, has been cast down."[73]

---

[71] Isaiah 14:13-17
[72] John 4:23
[73] Revelation 12:10

Those angels remaining in Heaven now fell down and began to worship and thank their God, and sang songs to His glory saying:

"Great and marvelous are Your works,

  Lord God Almighty!

Just and true are Your ways,

  O King of the saints!

Who shall not fear You, O Lord,

  and glorify Your name?

For You alone are holy.

  For all nations shall come and

  worship before You,

For Your judgments have been manifested."[74]

---

[74] Revelation 15:3-4

Creation Groans

In a flash like lightning, Satan was finally a prince, though not in Heaven. His kingdom was merely that of the air,[75] which didn't satiate his appetite of pride any more than it satisfies the human need for food.

Enraged, he raised a fist to Heaven, kicked the dust, and began to curse, "How dare You?!? I will ascend! Do You hear me?!? I will have Your throne!" His logic now compromised, he began to act schizophrenic, one moment raging like a beast, the next whimpering like a wounded puppy, then laughing like a lunatic, and so forth. "Ichabod! Ichabod!!! Cast down to Earth! Surrounded by the stench of mankind! Pee yew! Icky dirty little men! Ha ha! Yucky! I *hate* this place! I hate it!!! 'It's always about location, location, location!' Ha ha! Neighbors with man! Bosom pals! Ha ha! I *hate* them! I must steal! I must kill! I must destroy!"

One third of Heaven's hosts were also cast

---

[75] Ephesians 2:2

down.[76] Now realizing the severity of their error, some began to turn against their new prince. But like every tyrant in history, Satan would suffer no hint of revolt. His wrath was quickly and severely loosed upon the mutineers as his wickedness burned his rivals like briers and thorns.[77] None dared oppose him, and so all pledged their allegiance under his fearsome penalties. Thus began the cycle that would be imprinted upon human history, that every dictator who promises liberty only produces vicious bondage. The fallen angels had known true freedom only when serving in Heaven, but it was now only sickening irony that they had used their freedom to choose the bondage of Satan.

With his lordship established over Heaven's traitors, Satan now paced and planned His insane purpose. "I know what to do, and I know how to do it! I will present Elohim the reality of His error! I will prove that His plan is flawed! I will pollute His lovely Creation and program His filthy little man-apes to do it! I will introduce humanity to the pleasures of sin!"

---

[76] Revelation 12:4
[77] Isaiah 9:18

Satan still possessed his musical gifts, but now began to sing in the discordant tones that best expressed his wickedness.

"Come O man, the piper plays,

    And summons all the rats,

Come outside your garden walls,

    And see what I will catch!

Freedom from your liberty,

    I'll bind you for your choice!

Choose to lose your liberty,

    And make your final choice!

We'll dance until the sun should rise,

    But 'nevermore' you'll hear,

We'll jump and sing and play and ride,

    Forevermore you'll fear!

You've tasted the forbidden fruit,

    So come along and see,

The leaves, and bark, and dirt and root:

    The whole forbidden tree!

Sins of the heart will blind your eyes:

    Pride, hatred, lust, and greed.

Sins of the spirit bind your mind:

    False religion, and idolatry.

Sins of the flesh your soul confine:

Adultery and drunkenness,

Sins of omission will surprise:

Presumption, ignorance, and laziness."

And although mankind had known God, they did not glorify Him as God, nor were they thankful. But they became futile in their thoughts, and their foolish hearts were darkened.[78] Having eaten of the Tree of Knowledge, they became wise in their own eyes.[79] And professing to be wise, they became fools.[80]

As generations of men lived and died, the whole of creation began to suffer, and proclaimed the spiritual condition of mankind. Mingled with the good fruits of the earth, poisonous herbs now grew. Life-giving plants now struggled against fruitless weeds. The enormous creatures that man had ruled began to terrorize him, and man was forced to slay the dragons.[81] Sweet waters became embittered,[82] lush landscapes became deserts, and man had to dig deep

---

[78] Romans 1:21

[79] Proverbs 3:7; Proverbs 26:12; Isaiah 5:21

[80] Romans 1:22

[81] Psalms 91:13

[82] Exodus 15:23

wells to survive.[83] From somewhere in the heart of Earth came a groaning from nature for the undeserved curse it bore.[84] Mountains began to spew forth their deep wells of magma, scorching the heavenly scenery into pictures of hell. It was as if the planet knew that its king had changed, and began to prepare itself as his kingdom. Or perhaps man's temporal estate was merely foreshadowing his eternity: Earth's heavenly Eden now resembled hell's smoke, fire, and sulfurous fume.

---

[83] Genesis 26:18; Isaiah 12:2-3
[84] Romans 8:19-22; Genesis 3:17b

The Heavenly Offensive

God looked down from Heaven to see if there would be anyone among the children of men who would choose to seek Him, but not one was found that did not turn aside after Satan's temptations of the flesh; not one did good.[85] Occasional heroes of faith would arise on the Earth, but even these would have their stumbles and falls. Noah, Job, Abraham, Isaac, David: all these had relationship with Elohim, and yet all failed that relationship at some time or another. Not one of the sons of men was able to redeem himself with his own righteousness.

It was an act of mercy that Elohim accepted a scapegoat as payment for a debt of sins.[86] But He began to reveal an even deeper love for mankind as He told the angels, "I have given my Law to mankind, and have allowed the penalty of their sins to be paid with blood."[87]

---

[85] Psalms 14:2-3; 53:2-3
[86] Genesis 3:21; Leviticus 16:26-27; Hebrews 9:22
[87] Hebrews 10:4

Michael praised Him, "Yes, Lord! Your goodness and lovingkindness are made perfect in your mercy!" Others began to praise and worship, and then all would silence themselves as different angels began to sing their own new songs.

Aviel having found a new sense of completeness in the Lord began to worship Him:

"Lord, what grace You've shown exalts Your throne,

And causes my heart to sing,

The forgiven soul ever longs to see

The beauty of Your visage.

We angels see and know Your love,

But man must walk in faith,

So I praise and honor You with songs,

And love towards Your saints."

There was a generous applause and worship as he subsided, and even Kupi was heard to shout, "I agree!"

Another angel named Joamuel raised his voice and spoke these praises:

"Your majesty shines

Like the glory of summer

Warmth that never ends."

With a brief pause, he began again:

"I give gratitude

The least that I can return,

Your goodness abounds

And causes my heart to sing,

How glorious are Your ways!"

More praise was offered, and Kupi laughed as he said, "Lord, I think he was saying 'Praise You' with a *haiku*, and 'Thank Ya' with a *tanka*!" Rapturous laughter burst forth, and slowly faded. Suddenly from the back, a usually quiet angel named Netauel started to sing out what seemed to be a complex melody:

"You crafted Creation in beauty,

Your glory is seen in all You touch,

You delighted to see all complete.

Your love transcends all of the heavens,

Yet You care for perishing sparrows,

And how much more the sons of Adam?

When mankind rejected Your friendship,

You forgave for each sacrifice made,

And with three threes I give triune praise.'[88]

---

[88] The poem is three stanzas of three lines, and each line is three times three syllables.

The melody and rhythm were more moving to the mind than the heart, and yet what it lacked in musicality it seemed to possess in profundity. Some angels applauded while others smiled confusedly. Some tried to sound convincing as they encouraged their colleague with words like, "That was nice...really, it was! Did you make that up yourself?" One angel reassuringly said, "He's made each with differing gifts that ought to be used!"[89] And another jokingly added, "Or not!" And the laughter in Heaven could not be restrained. Even the clever writer himself was frolicsome and light, for there was no bad intent. For all of the angels that missed the significance of Netauel's composition, Kupi seemed to fully comprehend it, and was even moved to worship with joyful tears. All others were astonished when Elohim beamed a warm smile toward Netauel and said, "I bless your praise with all the height, width, and depth wherewith it was given!"[90] And all Heaven once more applauded and worshiped.

Elohim raised a hand for silence, and continued

---

[89] Romans 12:6
[90] Ephesians 3:18

His dissertation. "Although mankind can be saved by the Law,[91] I still desire more grace for my beloved.[92] It grieves my heart that men should suffer under the weight of their conscience even after their sins are covered.[93] Therefore, I want to give a sacrifice that is more perfect, that can even cleanse the *conscience*!"[94]

Angels began to wonder among themselves, "Man's conscience is *supposed* to suffer under sin. Is it even *possible* to have it cleansed?"

Elohim answered, "The cleansing of the conscience *can* be done, but only if the sacrifice is *perfect* by *My* standards." One angel was heard to say, "Well, then I guess it's not possible, for there's no sacrifice on Earth that is *really perfect*."

Elohim continued to reveal His plan and said, "I will go and be born as a man, and I will sacrifice *Myself* so that man's conscience can be cleansed, as well as his sins." All Heaven fell completely silent for a moment as Elohim spoke in claps of thunder, "The

---

[91] Hebrews 9:13
[92] Hosea 6:6; James 4:6
[93] Hebrews 9:14
[94] Hebrews 9:15: "for this reason"

time has come!" Then the praises of Heaven's hosts echoed even to the doorstep of hell, and Satan felt a shiver of fear though he did not yet know why.[95]

So God sent forth His Son to be born of a virgin,[96] and thus launched the greatest Heavenly Offensive of all time. Preparations had been long in the works, and prophets had spoken through the inspiration of the Holy Spirit of the coming Christ many hundreds of Earth-years before His arrival.[97] But for all of the prophesies, details, and perfection in Christ's arrival, God's plan was simple:[98] the bridge of salvation would be built by Christ, and the vehicle to cross would be man's freedom to choose. Inherent in this freedom is man's desire to be free. This was the threat that Satan felt so acutely. This was the bruise so tender to the touch of the Great Tyrant, and every tyrant since.

---

[95] 1 Corinthians 2:7-8
[96] Galatians 4:4-5; Isaiah 7:14
[97] John 5:46; Luke 24:27; 2 Peter 1:21
[98] 2 Corinthians 11:3

The Unended Battle for Souls

Freedom so freely given shook the very foundations of Satan's *modus operandi*: to bind and destroy the hearts, lives, and souls of mankind. But God's strategy was more powerful: to proclaim liberty to the captives, to offer consolation and joy for the spiritually deficient and heavy burdened.[99] In His compassion, Christ would *teach them*,[100] and they would become His workmanship[101]—his bondservants in love.[102] Thus God had declared, "I am Peace, and I am Eternal Life, and so shall peace and eternal life be given to all who are loyal to my kingdom! If they will choose to place their trust in Me, I will freely give them My living water welling up within their souls, and they will never thirst again![103] And I will freely give them the Tree of Life.[104] If they

---

[99] Isaiah 61:1
[100] Mark 6:34
[101] Ephesians 2:10
[102] Deuteronomy 15:16-17
[103] John 7:38; Revelation 22:17
[104] Revelation 22:14

will choose to be free through faith in Me, then I will make them free indeed!"[105] If the enemies of Heaven would have known God's strategy in advance, they would not have crucified Christ.[106]

Satan wasn't content to have paved a *broad* way to damnation that would cause *most* people to lose their souls. "No!" he cried! "I want *all* souls to be damned! *Not one* shall escape without a fight! *Not one* shall be rescued from my clutches without a hellish assault! I am War, and I am Murder, and so shall war and murder befall those who betray my tyranny!"

A God with unfailing love, and an adversary with unquenchable hatred; one viewing the souls of mankind as His children, and the other as his conquest; one too merciful to leave us to destruction, and the other too relentless to allow us to be saved. From this chemistry war emerged, for only war can emerge when madmen diametrically oppose righteousness and freedom. Satan's battle against Heaven was quickly lost even as it began. But his war against mankind and his desire to oppress great and

---

[105] John 8:36
[106] 1 Corinthians 2:8

small will never end until the Old Serpent is cast into the Lake of Fire.[107] Thus the war that began in Heaven has since continued on Earth. And the fighting for souls wages hotly about us all, even as you are reading this now.

---

[107] Revelation 20:2,10

Our Part In The Battle

While this book might seem merely fantasy to some, it is a terrific reality that there is a God who loves us, a devil who hates us, and a choice that we must make between the two. Jesus Christ often taught about a literal Heaven and a literal hell,[108] and that "whosoever *will*" could make Heaven their eternal home through a *personal choice* to follow Him.[109] He also taught that only those that actively obeyed and followed Him would be saved.[110] Furthermore, Christ taught that if we do not choose *for* Him—if we merely hope to chance that we will make it to Heaven—we have in fact chosen against Him,[111] and our souls will be lost for eternity.

It is my prayer that you would personally receive the unfailing love that God has for you, and that you

---

[108] Matthew 7:19; Matthew 10:28; Matthew 22:13; Matthew 23:33; Mark 9:43-48; Luke 12:5

[109] Matthew 16:25; 20:26-27; Mark 8:34-35; 10:43; Luke 9:5, 24; John 3:16-18; Revelation 22:17

[110] John 3:3,7; Matthew 7:21-23

[111] Luke 11:23

would begin to experience the goodness that He has purposed for your life.[112] It is the prayer of faith that saves, heals, and delivers,[113] so I have included this prayer as a guideline for those who would like to choose to begin following Christ now. I encourage you to believe and pray this:

> *"Jesus, I admit that I am a sinner.*[114]
>
> *I believe that You are Lord of all, that You died for my sins, and that You rose again to give me life.*[115] *I ask You to forgive my sins,*[116] *and to come into my heart.*[117]
>
> *Make me a new person,*[118] *in Jesus' name,*[119] *Amen.*

If you prayed this prayer, or you would like more information about following Christ, please contact me through my website:

www.elkidwell.com

---

[112] Jeremiah 29:11-13

[113] James 5:15; Romans 10:10

[114] 1 John 1:9

[115] Romans 5:8; 10:9

[116] Colossians 1:13-14; 1 John 1:9

[117] Revelation 3:20

[118] Psalms 51:10; 2 Corinthians 5:17

[119] John 14:13-14; John 16:26-27

Epilogue

Of the oldest known societies in history, it is remarkable that mankind seems to instinctively organize himself into a hierarchy. This is especially remarkable when considering the similarity of governments of tribes and nations on opposite sides of our world which had no direct influence or communication. Surely, this cannot be mere coincidence, but is evidence of the work of an eternal Creator who has imprinted some of His eternal knowledge and character into His creation.[120]

Jesus Christ revealed that the pattern of hierarchical leadership is God's design as seen in the members of the Trinity.[121] The Bible describes God as a triune being[122] consisting of the distinct persons of the Father, the Son, and the Holy Spirit,[123] joined in

---

[120] Ecclesiastes 3:11b

[121] John 14:10

[122] This book literalizes the personalities of the Trinity for clarity and illustration, not as support for tritheism.

[123] Matthew 28:19; Galatians 4:6

the single being of God.[124] Christ often stated that he was a willing subordinate to His Father, and even the Holy Spirit[125]—He temporarily sacrificed His celestial equality to become a man so that we could be saved.[126] He was restored to a greater glory after His resurrection, thereby availing the opportunity of our resurrection to glory.[127] So as we were created in God's image, our instinctive systems of hierarchical leadership and government can be deduced to have come from God.

Now let's consider, if all of the citizens of Heaven and Earth were automatons, why would God have instituted a government of ranks? If all beings were fated and their destinies simply predestined—if God's will *just happened*—then making them subordinate to the authority of others would be as ridiculous as the blind leading the blind. Therefore, it is obvious that God instituted a chain of command in Heaven

---

[124] The singularity of the three persons of the Trinity is an Essential doctrine of Christianity, as is their distinct personalities. See Ephesians 1:3-13.

[125] John 5:19,30; 8:28; 14:10; Matthew 4:1

[126] Psalms 8:5; Hebrews 2:7-9

[127] Hebrews 2:9

because the angels were indeed created with a free will. And these ranks must have been implemented for the purpose of warfare that the Lord had apparently foreseen. For example, in Joshua 5:14, Joshua is visited by the "Commander (or Captain) of the army of the Lord." Regardless of whether or not this was actually Christ, one thing is certain: God's ranks were militant in nature. What purpose would there be in having an angelic captain or a sergeant[128] if the subordinate angels had no choice but to obey? The very title of the Captain of the Lord's Hosts would be a contradiction to God's perfection if God's Creation had no free will. It is upon these premises that we must realize that our salvation is dependent upon the choice of our will, and not the whims or so-called "predestination" of God's will.

As a believer in the inerrancy and authoritativeness of scripture, I have strummed softly while composing this piece. I confess to have taken liberties when "reading between the lines" in certain parts of scripture, but have been careful to not

---

[128] Joshua 5:14

compromise the essential doctrines of the Christian faith (such as salvation by grace through faith, and redemption through the blood of Christ). But in some instances, falsehoods are deliberately stated by Lucifer—he was a murderer and a liar from the beginning[129]—or other evil spirits.

Although scripture is inerrant, I am not. Therefore, it is my prayer that this tale may provoke you into a greater awareness of the intense and endless hatred God's adversary feels against mankind. But most importantly, that you may have a deeper appreciation of the great love of God for humanity, the sacrifice of His only begotten Son, and a true relationship with the living and powerful Word of God[130] and the Word become flesh, Jesus Christ.[131]

---

[129] John 8:44
[130] Hebrews 4:12
[131] Hebrews 4:12; John 1:14

About the Author

E. L. Kidwell has been a Christian since 1982. He also busies himself as a husband, father, pastor, Bible student, software engineer, graphic designer, and musician. He loves classic literature which he has described as "an addiction which often consumes the hours when I should be sleeping." He is a lover of the Holy Bible, and believes that it is the authoritative Word of God and the "power of God to salvation for everyone who believes."

Other titles from Kidwell Publishing available through your favorite bookstore or online at: www.kidwellpublishing.com

The Pilgrim's Progress – Part I and Part II
By John Bunyan
ISBN: 978-0-9817634-3-9

This timeless class of John Bunyan "delivered under the similtude of a dream" captures the hearts and minds of readers with Bunyan's depth of understanding and scriptural knowledge, as well as his subtle comedy and witticisms.

This edition contains both parts of Bunyan's tale, including all of the original scripture references in an easy-to-read format.

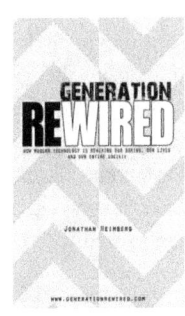

Generation Rewired
By Jonathan Heimberg
ISBN: 978-0-9817634-2-2

Generation Rewired is an informative look into the world of technology, and how it is subtly changing the way we work, live and think. Examining the social networking phenomenon and other pervasive technologies, this book is an eye-opening, quick read that will thoroughly change the way you view technology.

Christian Living:
Encouragement for Growing Christians
By E. L. Kidwell
ISBN: 978-0-9817634-0-8

Like the body, the soul needs a healthy diet to grow. And an essential nutrient for spiritual growth is encouragement! This book contains a collection of messages on relevant issues to help every growing Christian be all they can be in Christ. This book is categorized topically for use as a Bible study guide, devotional help, or for spiritual reference.

(continued)

Offering Stories, Quotes, and Illustrations
By Robert Polaco
ISBN: 978-0-9817634-5-3

This book is a compilation of over 200 offering stories, quotes, and illustrations. Each illustration also contains a note line where pastors or administrators can indicate the date on which the illustration was used, preventing the potential embarrassment of reusing an illustration. This is a must have companion for any pastor or church administrator.

The Labyrinth of Shadow
By Aly Lyn
ISBN: 978-0-9817634-4-6

Peace was predicted in the ancient writings, and a rising power claimed lordship of all the lands. After seven years of tranquility, the people have been lulled into a false state of security. Forgotten in the ancient writings was the warning of what else would come. Enter the Labyrinth of Shadow, an exciting world of fantastic creatures, and action-packed adventure!

www.ingramcontent.com/pod-product-compliance
Lightning Source LLC
Chambersburg PA
CBHW051308170626
46809CB00004B/1800